Woo-Hoo... Chris P. Is 2!

Happy Birthday!

Len Lucero and **Kristina Tracy**

illustrated by **Penny Weber**

HAY HOUSE, INC.
Carlsbad, California • New York City
London • Sydney • Johannesburg
Vancouver • Hong Kong • New Delhi

Published and distributed in the United States by: Hay House, Inc.: www.hayhouse.com® • **Published and distribued in Australia by:** Hay House Australia Pty. Ltd.: www.hayhouse.com .au • **Published and distributed in the United Kingdom by:** Hay House UK, Ltd.: www.hayhouse.co.uk • **Published and distributed in the Republic of South Africa by:** Hay House SA (Pty), Ltd.: www.hayhouse.co.za • **Distributed in Canada by:** Raincoast Books: www.raincoast.com • **Published in India by:** Hay House Publishers India: www.hayhouse.co.in

Editorial assistance and interior design: Jenny Richards • *Illustrations:* © Penny Weber • *Interior photos:* © Len Lucero

Library of Congress Control Number: 2015947477

Hardcover ISBN: 978-1-4019-4441-4

10 9 8 7 6 5 4 3 2 1

1st edition, November 2015

Printed in the United States of America

To Chris P. Bacon, the tiny little pig who has grown into a size big enough to fit his giant heart! Thank you for all the love, laughs, and inspiration you bring to me and everyone you meet!

— Len Lucero

Hi! It's me again . . . Chris P. Bacon. Guess what? Yesterday, I turned 2 and it was just about the best, most amazing day of my whole life!!

Can you believe it has been almost 2 years since my dad,
Len, adopted me, brought me to live on the farm with his
whole family, and made me my special cart? I have had lots
of fun and exciting days, but yesterday might have topped
them all—and I want to tell you all about it!

The day started out bright and early. I tried to sleep in, but I was too excited. No one else was up yet, so I started making a lot of noise, hoping to get someone's attention.

Finally, Dad came in singing "Happy Birthday" and carrying a tower of scrumptious pancakes.

I gobbled them down (big surprise!) and we headed outside to do our chores and say good morning to all my friends on the farm.

I finished all my chores . . . played tag with Aspen . . . had a few snacks . . . but it STILL was not time for the party. The clock moved way too slow.

AT LAST, Dad came to get me!

Wooo-hooo!

When I rolled into the barn, it was the most incredible sight! Lots of my friends and family (animal and human) were there. Even Joe the Bellman came all the way from New York City!

There were balloons and streamers,
all my favorite snacks, a yummy cake,
and even a Cheerio sculpture of ME!

I got tons of hugs and kisses and Happy Birthday wishes. We even made a conga line! Everyone had a great time!

Just when I thought the party couldn't get any better, Dad got up and asked if anyone wanted to tell a story about me.

The first one to raise his paw was Aspen, my best friend in the whole wide world! He hopped up onto a haystack and said . . .

Woof! . . . I can't believe it has been two years since Chris came to live with us. Who knew that a pig would be so much fun? Ever since I watched him learn to roll using his special cart, I knew that he was "yooo-neek"! He was so small, but so determined. We have been inseparable ever since.

Next up was Mr. and Mrs. Cluckingham. They told a story about me saving the day!

Bok, bok, bok . . . Chris P. Bacon is one helpful pig to have around! Last summer our mischievous little chicks got themselves into a jam. They ended up stuck out in the middle of the pond with no way to get back. Without a second thought, Chris used his cart and pulled our babies to safety. Happy Birthday, Chris, you are the best!

Next came a good friend of mine—a little girl named Anna, who I met at an ice cream shop way back when I was 1. She visits me sometimes and we play together.

When I first met Chris, I had just started using my wheelchair. I was having trouble getting used to it and I felt so different from everyone else. Seeing Chris in his cart, and how happy and positive he was, helped me be the same way. The time that I spend with Chris is one of my favorite things!

My sister, Ashley, told a funny story about me.

One weekend we were getting ready for a bake sale to raise money for the animal shelter. Mom and I had made tons of treats and set them out on the kitchen counter. Chris wandered into the kitchen and found the "feast," but did not see the "Bake Sale" sign that had slipped out of sight. Needless to say, there was hardly a crumb left once he was done. We still laugh about that day!

The last person to talk was Dad.

Ever since Chris came to live with our family, things have changed. I never thought I would be buying ten pounds of grapes each week! But that is a small price to pay for all the love, fun, and adventure Chris has brought into our lives. From the first day I brought him home, there has never been a dull moment. He is one of a kind, a great friend, and we all love him very much!

When the party was over, Dad carried me back to the house and tucked me in.

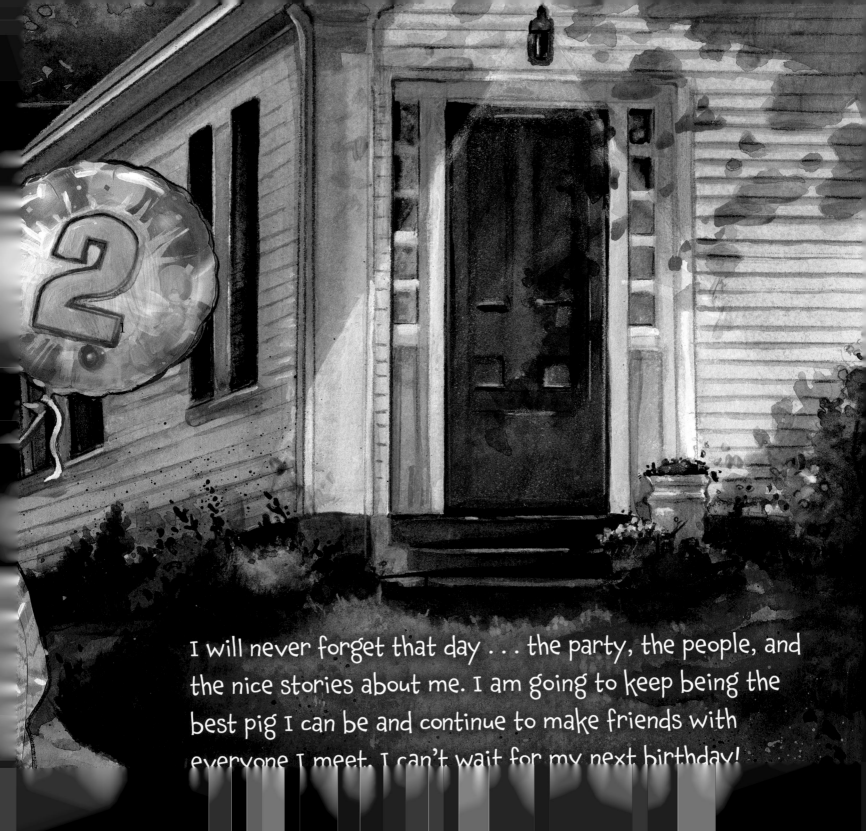

I will never forget that day . . . the party, the people, and the nice stories about me. I am going to keep being the best pig I can be and continue to make friends with everyone I meet. I can't wait for my next birthday!

THE BIG 2!

We hope you enjoyed this Hay House book. If you'd like to receive our online catalog featuring additional information on Hay House books and products, or if you'd like to find out more about the Hay Foundation, please contact:

Hay House, Inc.
P.O. Box 5100
Carlsbad, CA 92018-5100

(760) 431-7695 or (800) 654-5126
(760) 431-6948 (fax) or (800) 650-5115 (fax)
www.hayhouse.com® · www.hayfoundation.org

Published and distributed in Australia by: Hay House Australia Pty. Ltd., 18/36 Ralph St., Alexandria NSW 2015
Phone: 612-9669-4299 · Fax: 612-9669-4144 · www.hayhouse.com.au

Published and distributed in the United Kingdom by: Hay House UK, Ltd., Astley House, 33 Notting Hill Gate, London W11 3JQ
Phone: 44-20-3675-2450 · Fax: 44-20-3675-2451 · www.hayhouse.co.uk

Published and distributed in the Republic of South Africa by: Hay House SA (Pty), Ltd.,
P.O. Box 990, Witkoppen 2068 · info@hayhouse.co.za · www.hayhouse.co.za

Published in India by: Hay House Publishers India, Muskaan Complex, Plot No. 3, B-2, Vasant Kunj,
New Delhi 110 070 · Phone: 91-11-4176-1620 · Fax: 91-11-4176-1630 · www.hayhouse.co.in

Distributed in Canada by: Raincoast Books, 2240 Viking Way, Richmond, B.C. V6V 1N2
Phone: (604) 633-5714 · Fax: (604) 565-3770 · www.raincoast.com